THE SECRET EXPLORERS®
AND THE TOMB ROBBERS

CONTENTS

Chapter One
BACK IN TIME

I love it when the museum is busy! thought Gustavo. All around him, people were admiring statues and peering into glass cases full of amazing objects from the past. He straightened his "Volunteer" armband.

"Excuse me!" called a cheery woman in a blue jacket. She pointed to a globe-shaped vase. It was black and decorated with cream swirls. "Do you know how old this is?" she asked.

"It's probably about a thousand years old," Gustavo replied. "It was made by the Marajoara people. They lived on an island at the end of the Amazon River, right here in Brazil."

"That's really interesting," said the woman. "Thanks for your help!"

"No problem," said Gustavo with a grin.

The museum was close to his Rio de Janeiro home, so he'd been coming as long as he could remember. He knew so much about the objects on display that he could answer any question the visitors asked! He loved history and enjoyed helping to care for the artefacts other civilizations had left behind. *It would be so amazing to go back in time*, Gustavo thought, *and see these objects being used by real ancient people!*

Out of the corner of his eye, he noticed a light shimmering. Gustavo's heart leaped. *Could it be...?* He turned around. On the lift door was a glowing circle with the letters N, E, S and W. A compass!

Gustavo knew what it meant – a new mission for the Secret Explorers!

He hurried to the lift, tingling with

excitement. The doors slid open by themselves and Gustavo stepped inside. All around him was a brilliant white light.

Wind whipped around Gustavo. It made him feel as if he was whizzing through the brightness. Then a moment later the light faded. Gustavo was back at the Exploration Station!

It had gleaming black stone walls, a map of the world on the floor, and a huge picture of the Milky Way on the ceiling. There was a line of computers along one wall.

"Gustavo – here!" he called.

A girl wearing a leaf-green T-shirt and a boy with red hair jumped up from a squishy sofa. They both grinned.

"Hi Leah," said Gustavo. "Hi Ollie!"

"I was just showing Ollie my new book about beetles," said Leah. She was the Biology Explorer, and knew all about plants and animals. Ollie was wearing a shirt with a parrot pattern – he was the team's rainforest expert.

Soon the other Secret Explorers arrived 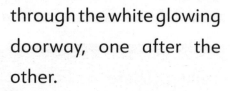 through the white glowing doorway, one after the other.

A girl skateboarded in. "Kiki – here!" She was the Engineering Explorer, and had made the skateboard herself.

"Cheng – here!" He was passionate about rocks and volcanoes.

Next came a girl with short dark hair who knew everything about dinosaurs. "Tamiko – here!"

"Roshni – here!" said the Space Explorer. She glanced up at the Milky Way on the ceiling.

"Connor – here!" said the ocean expert.

They all gathered excitedly around the map on the floor. Gustavo felt a swirl of

excitement in his middle. The Exploration Station would soon tell them about the mission!

"Where will it be?" Cheng wondered. His eyes sparkled as he watched the map.

"There!" Connor pointed. "Near the Mediterranean Sea!"

A pinpoint of light had appeared on the map. It grew and shimmered.

"The mission's in Egypt!" said Gustavo. "Right beside the River Nile!"

A screen projected up from the map. It showed the inside of a museum, and a man and woman in smart uniforms. *They must be the curators who work there*, Gustavo thought. He listened eagerly to what they were saying.

"We just don't get enough visitors," the woman said sadly. She dusted a glass case containing a scarab beetle made of blue stone. *"This amulet from Pharaoh Khufu's pyramid is our only real treasure. But it's not enough to bring people in."*

The man sighed. *"You're right,"* he said. *"If only Khufu's treasures hadn't been looted by tomb robbers, we'd have a much better display."*

"We don't have any choice," the woman said. *"We'll have to close down the museum..."*

The screen disappeared.

The Secret Explorers looked at each other, wide-eyed.

"Our mission must be to save the museum," said Ollie.

Roshni pointed to Gustavo. "It's your mission! Your badge is glowing."

Gustavo felt a rush of excitement. He adored museums. *We can't let the one in Egypt close down!* he thought.

"That makes sense," said Tamiko. "You're the History Explorer, after all."

"Hey, my badge is glowing," said Kiki. "I wonder how engineering can help the museum?"

"We know the Exploration Station always chooses the right team," said Leah.

"True!" agreed Kiki. She went over to the computers and pressed a button. A hatch in the floor opened and up rose the Beagle. It looked like an old go-kart, with two battered seats and a wonky steering wheel. *But it won't stay like that*, Gustavo thought.

The Beagle was named after the ship that carried a famous scientist, Charles Darwin, on a voyage of discovery. What were he and Kiki going to discover? Gustavo couldn't wait to find out!

Everyone took their places at the computer screens while he and Kiki climbed onto the Beagle. Gustavo pressed the "GO" button. The Beagle shook and rattled as if it was falling apart. The wheels disappeared and wooden panels rose around them. In a flash of light, the Beagle jerked forwards. Gustavo clutched the sides. They whooshed

through dazzling whiteness, then after a few moments the light faded. The Beagle was bobbing gently up and down – on water!

"It's transformed into a boat! We're on a river!" said Gustavo.

Kiki's eyes shone. "It must be the Nile!"

Gustavo shaded his eyes from the hot sun and looked to shore. Two gigantic, triangular

white shapes gleamed in the heat. "You're right!" he gasped. "Those are pyramids!"

"Wow!" said Kiki. "They're bigger than I ever imagined! It's almost like they're touching the sky."

Gustavo's eyes grew wide. "Hang on, there are supposed to be three pyramids... and one of these is only half finished..." His tummy did a flip. "Kiki... we've gone back in time – to ancient Egypt!"

Chapter Two
RESCUE ON THE NILE

"This is fantastic!" said Gustavo, leaping up. "I've always wanted to see an ancient civilization – and now I'm in ancient Egypt, on the River Nile!"

Kiki clutched the side of the Beagle, which was wobbling about. "We'll be *in* the Nile if you don't sit down," she said. "But Gustavo, are you sure this is *really* ancient Egypt?"

Gustavo watched, spellbound, as two fishermen pulled a net full of splashing fish ashore. Nearby, a girl was washing her hair at the water's edge. People in tunics and sandals sat in the doorways of white flat-roofed houses, or in the shade of rustling palm trees.

He grinned at Kiki. "I'm sure. We're in the time of the pharaohs – the rulers of ancient Egypt!"

"Awesome!" Kiki said. "But how will being in ancient Egypt help us save the museum? It doesn't even exist yet."

Gustavo sat down on a wooden bench.

"The Exploration Station must have sent us here for a reason. Let's go and find out what it is."

A flapping noise made him look up. A square-shaped sail billowed open above them.

"The Beagle wants to set off too," Gustavo said. "But I have no idea how to sail a boat!"

"I'll figure it out!" Kiki twanged a rope attached to the sail. "Okay, the sail moves like that..." She shifted to where a large oar was fastened to the back of the boat. "And this is a sort of rudder, for steering..."

Gustavo explored the Beagle too. Tucked under the bench was what looked like a tool box. Gustavo opened it up, and the Beagle gave a burst of excited electronic beeps.

They sounded very out of place on the ancient Nile.

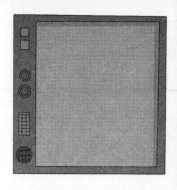

"Hush," Gustavo said with a laugh. "We don't want anyone to realise we're from the future!" He saw that the lid of the box was a screen, with a microphone and a row of buttons. "It's a communications panel," he told Kiki.

"Brilliant!" Kiki said. "That means we can call the Exploration Station if we need help."

"Even though they're thousands of years ahead of us," added Gustavo. "You're amazing, Beagle!"

The Beagle gave a smug beep.

Gustavo found a waterproof bag tucked by the communications panel. It contained tunics, belts, and sandals. "We'd better put these on before we meet any ancient

Egyptians," he said. "They might find our jeans and trainers a bit strange."

After they had changed, Kiki held tightly to the ropes that controlled the sail while Gustavo took hold of the rudder. The wind filled the sail and the Beagle glided along the Nile.

They both looked up in awe as they drew closer to the pyramids. They were so huge, the people dotted around them looked as tiny as ants. There were smaller buildings and walls around them too. "I never knew the pyramids were white," said Kiki. "I always thought they were the colour of sand."

"They're covered with polished limestone," said Gustavo. "By our time, the limestone will have gone, and pollution will have made the stone blocks undernearth turn darker."

Kiki pointed to a giant statue. It looked like a resting lion, but with a human head. "Hey, isn't that the Great Sphinx? I've seen pictures of it, but it didn't have a nose."

"It broke off," Gustavo said. He was so excited to see the Sphinx with a complete face! "No one knows what happened to it. And there's an Anubis!"

He pointed to a statue standing among the various buildings. The statue had a human body and a head similar to a dog's.

"Was Anubis one of the pharaohs?" asked Kiki.

Gustavo shook his head. "He was one of the gods worshipped by the ancient Egyptians," he said. "They believed he was in charge of death and the afterlife."

"He's got a jackal's head," said Kiki. "I've seen those at home in Ghana... Hold on, the wind's changed direction!"

Kiki pulled on a rope to swing the sail around. Gustavo adjusted the rudder and the Beagle picked up speed. Ahead was a wooden dock jutting out into the river. A large ship was moored there. Gustavo saw that the ship's decks were stacked with blocks of stone.

"Those are for building the pyramid," he said.

Dozens of men were unloading the stones. Several more walked up and down, shouting orders. The men used long poles to move the blocks onto ramps.

"They're using the poles as levers," said Kiki. "Levers increase the amount of force you're able to create, which is why they can lift those massive lumps of stone." She grinned. "It's ancient engineering!"

A small boat was coming towards them, rowed by a boy about their own age. He was surrounded by packages and bags stuffed with scrolls. He suddenly stopped rowing

and started scooping water out of his boat
with a wooden bucket.

"Great goddess Bastet!" the boy
exclaimed, looking up at the sky. "Can't you
stop the water coming in?"

"Hey!" Kiki yelled. "Do you need help?"

"Yes!" the boy shouted. "All my stuff's
going to get soaked!"

Gustavo steered the Beagle until they
were alongside the boy's boat. He leaned
over the side and used his hands to help
scoop the water out.

"Thanks for helping," the boy gasped.

"I'm worried that the honey Mum wanted will end up at the bottom of the Nile!"

"What's your boat made of?" Kiki asked.

The boy stared. "Papyrus, of course."

Kiki looked confused.

"It's a kind of paper," Gustavo whispered. "Ancient Egyptians made it from reeds."

"Perfect," Kiki said. She rummaged under the bench on the Beagle and pulled out a wooden bowl. "Your mum's honey," she said to the boy. "Can I use some? And one of those scrolls? I need them to patch up your boat!"

"How can honey mend the hole?" wondered the boy, but he passed over a small jar made from pottery and a papyrus scroll.

Working quickly, Kiki poured some honey into the

bowl. She unrolled the scroll and used her fingers to smear the paste all over it. Then she climbed into the boy's boat and pressed it firmly over the hole.

"It's not perfect," she said, "but it should hold until you reach the dock."

The boy grinned with relief. "Amazing! Thank you so much!"

Kiki climbed back into the Beagle and they followed the boy into the dock, just in case Kiki's papyrus patch sprang a leak. Once both boats were tied up, Gustavo and Kiki helped the boy unload his scrolls and packages.

"I'm really glad you were on the Nile today," the boy

said. "My name's Bek." His head was shaved except for one lock of hair on the side. He had a battered leather bag slung across his body.

"I'm Kiki," Kiki told him, "and this is Gustavo."

"Those aren't Egyptian names," said Bek. "Where are you from?"

"A long way away," said Gustavo. "We're from... er... Discoveria."

The boy tilted his head, looking puzzled. Before he could ask any more questions, Kiki said, "Shall we help you carry your stuff home?"

"That would be great!" said Bek delightedly. Once he'd handed them some bags filled with scrolls, he heaped everything else into his bag, picked up a big sack of flour, and set off.

Gustavo and Kiki followed. They passed people moving more stone blocks, merchants carrying bread and linen, and children playing with toy wooden crocodiles.

"Let's keep an eye out for clues about our mission," Gustavo whispered to Kiki.

Kiki nodded. "Maybe helping Bek will somehow help the museum."

They passed the statue of Anubis with its strange jackal head. A shadow flickered beside it, and Gustavo had the feeling he was being watched. He spun round to

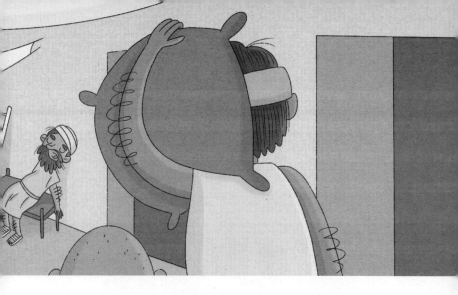

look – and saw a tall woman in a long white shawl that swooped behind her. But the next moment, she had gone.

Bek glanced at him. "Are you okay?" he asked.

"I thought someone was following us," Gustavo said. "But I must have imagined it..."

Chapter Three
STOLEN!

Bek's home was larger than the ones along the riverbank. Its flat roof had a canopy, making a shady area to sit. Gustavo knew that the family would sleep up there on hot nights.

"It seems to be built of bricks," Kiki whispered, sounding surprised. "And the windows are tiny!"

"They're not like our bricks," Gustavo whispered back. "They're made of mud and straw. And the windows are small and high up, to keep out the heat and dust."

Bek led them up to the house. Three men hurried past, carrying armfuls of white linen. "They work for my grandfather," Bek explained. "He's a mummifier."

Gustavo felt a thrill of excitement. He knew the ancient Egyptians mummified the dead to preserve their bodies, because they believed they would need them in the afterlife.

"My grandfather was in charge of mummifying Pharaoh Khufu's body," said Bek. "See the biggest pyramid? Khufu's mummy is buried in there."

Kiki nudged Gustavo. "The people from the museum spoke about Khufu," she whispered. "Maybe we're about to find out how to complete our mission!"

They followed Bek up a ramp, through the front door, and into a large room. There were shelves piled with scrolls. Blocks of ink stood on a table beside a stack of brushes.

"These are our writing materials," Bek explained, as they all put down their bags.

Kiki picked up some round objects. "What are these?" She sniffed them. "Mmm, they smell like cinnamon."

"They're incense pellets," said Bek. "I like to burn them while I practise writing. The scent helps me concentrate. Here, have a couple."

"Thanks!" Kiki tucked two incense pellets into her belt. "I'll use these when I'm building things."

Just then Gustavo's eye was caught by a sheet of papyrus on another table. On it were drawings of a frog and a bird. "Those are hieroglyphs, aren't they, Bek?" he said. "Egyptian writing?"

Bek was stacking scrolls in a basket woven from rushes. He glanced around.

"That's right. They look like pictures, but most of them stand for a sound. Don't you have hieroglyphs in Discoveria?"

"Where?" said Kiki.

Gustavo nudged her.

"Oh, right, Discoveria," she said. "No, we write with joined-up letters."

"So do I, in school," said Bek. "That's called hieratic writing, and it's quicker than

writing in hieroglyphs." He sighed. "But I really want to train to be a scribe, and write perfect hieroglyphs." He pulled a sheet of papyrus from a box under the table. "I'm learning, though. Look."

The papyrus was completely covered with Bek's attempts at hieroglyphs. Most were smudged, but Gustavo could make out birds, snakes, feathers and a lot of legs.

"I want to write as well as this," Bek said, taking a scroll from the back of a shelf. He unrolled it and Gustavo and Kiki leaned in to look. The scroll was covered in very neat, black and red hieroglyphs. There was a drawing of a pyramid at the top, then rows of hieroglyphs beneath. Gustavo recognised a leg, a hippo and what looked like a pair of doorways.

"What does it say?" wondered Kiki.

Bek glanced around, as if he was making sure no one was listening. He whispered, "It's a code. It says where the entrance to Pharaoh Khufu's pyramid is hidden. It must be kept secret, so no one breaks in to steal his treasures."

"What kinds of treasures?" Kiki asked.

"Everything he needs for the afterlife," Bek explained. "Baskets and bowls of food, clothes, jars of wine and oil... Khufu has two boats buried near the pyramid, too."

"Model boats?" said Gustavo. He'd seen pictures of small wooden boats that were buried in ancient Egyptian tombs.

"They're in pieces, but they're full-size ones," said Bek.

"Wow!" said Gustavo and Kiki together.

"There'll be a *lot* of gold and jewels in there too," said Bek, "and–"

A shadow fell across the doorway. They all turned to see a tall woman wearing a shoulder-length black wig, decorated with beads. A long white shawl hung around her shoulders.

Gustavo drew a sharp breath. It was the woman

he'd seen hiding behind the statue of Anubis! *I didn't imagine her*, he thought.

Behind her was a man wearing a wraparound skirt, like a kilt. There was another woman, too – she wore a long tunic, and her hair was short and scruffy.

Bek smiled at the tall woman. "Are you looking for my father?"

"No, I'm not," she replied. She snatched up the papyrus from the table, sending the stones tumbling.

One of them landed on the man's foot. He yelped.

"Quiet, Yuf!" The woman waved the papyrus in Bek's shocked face. "This is what I want – the instructions for getting into the pyramid!"

The scruffy woman giggled. "We're going to get the treasure! We're going to get the treasure!" she chanted.

"Bunefer!" the tall woman snapped. "Stop it!"

Gustavo leaped forward to snatch the papyrus back. But the woman whipped it aside and pushed past him.

"Yuf! Bunefer! Let's go," she called.

"Yes, Nebet. Coming, Nebet," said the man.

The scruffy woman glared at Gustavo. "Don't follow us, or..."

"Right now, Bunefer!" Nebet shouted.

And they were gone.

Bek looked horrified. "Now they can get into Pharaoh Khufu's tomb and steal his treasures. It's all my fault!"

"You couldn't help it," Kiki said gently.

"You don't understand," said Bek. His eyes were wide with worry. "If anyone finds out they've got that papyrus, Grandad will be in big trouble."

"Bek!" a voice called. "Bek, I need your help shifting these jars!"

"That's him now," said Bek. "What if he finds out the papyrus has been stolen?"

Kiki squeezed his arm. "Go and help your grandad," she said. "We'll fix this."

"Thank you," Bek said. "May the gods bring you luck!" He disappeared into the next room.

Kiki and Gustavo huddled together.

"Now we know what our mission is," Gustavo whispered excitedly. "We must stop that robbery, so the treasures stay safely in the tomb!"

"Yes!" said Kiki. "Then one day archaeologists can discover them, and they can be displayed in the museum. Imagine how many people will go to see them!"

Gustavo nodded. "We must save those treasures – and help Bek!"

Chapter Four
THE SECRET CODE

Gustavo and Kiki hurried back towards the pyramids. Gustavo gazed up at the largest one and thought of the incredible treasures hidden inside it. He and Kiki were the only ones who could stop Nebet and her gang from stealing them all. It seemed impossible.

"How do we even begin to stop the robbers?" he wondered.

"We need help," Kiki said. "Let's ask the Secret Explorers!"

They headed towards the Nile. Gustavo caught the scent of honey as they passed a line of donkeys laden with jars. They ran down the riverbank to the Beagle and jumped on board.

As their feet hit the deck, the Beagle beeped.

BIP-BIP-BIP-BIP! BIP-BIP!

Gustavo laughed. "We're pleased to see you, too!"

Kiki opened the box that held the communications equipment. As the screen burst into life, she spoke into the mic. "The Beagle to Exploration Station. Can you hear us?"

"Exploration Station to the Beagle. Tamiko here. Sending visual."

The screen flickered and all the Secret Explorers appeared on it.

The sight of their friends immediately made Gustavo feel more hopeful. He quickly explained what had happened. "So to save the museum, we must stop the robbers and make sure no one steals Khufu's treasures," he finished.

"Leah's calling up some pyramid info on her computer," said Cheng.

A moment later, Leah said, "The pyramid has got a few tunnels inside it. Some of them were possibly built to confuse robbers."

Gustavo nodded. "I remember reading about that. When a pyramid is finished being built, the builders block them off with rubble," he said. "That's to stop robbers getting in."

"I know!" said Connor. "Could you use rubble to seal up the treasure chamber?"

"That would work!" said Gustavo.

Kiki broke in. "We could stick the rubble

together with the mortar the builders use," she said. "If we build a wall across the treasure chamber entrance, the tomb will be safe."

"Great idea!" said Ollie. "But how are you going to get inside the pyramid? The entrance is secret, isn't it?"

Everybody at the Exploration Station turned to their computers, searching for a solution to the problem.

"Hold on," Gustavo said slowly. "You know that papyrus the gang stole? The one with the directions to the secret entrance? I think I remember the hieroglyphs on it. If we can work out what the code is..."

"Describe them," said Tamiko. "We'll look them up and translate."

"The first one's easy – that was the Sphinx," said Gustavo. "Then it was a sky with a star hanging from it..."

Tamiko's keyboard clacked. "That must mean sunset," she said.

"Then a pair of legs," Gustavo continued. "Then a... squiggly thing..."

"Like a question mark," Kiki chipped in, "but the wrong way round."

"The legs mean walk, and the curly thing's a hundred," said Tamiko. "It must mean walk a hundred paces."

"There was a hippopotamus too," said Gustavo. "What can that mean?"

"I would guess it means hippopotamus," said Tamiko with a giggle.

"I remember a yellow circle as well," said Kiki, "with lines coming down from it."

"Sunbeams," said Tamiko.

"But it was sort of crossed out," Kiki added.

"Oh. Maybe it was a mistake," said Tamiko.

"Then there was a person looking up," said Gustavo.

Tamiko frowned. "Hmm. Maybe it means you're supposed to look up too," she suggested.

"The last ones looked like two doorways,"

remembered Kiki. "Maybe that means the way into the pyramid?"

Tamiko typed quickly. "I think each doorway shape means the number ten," she said. "So both together mean twenty."

"I think that was all of them," said Gustavo. "Can you tell us them again?"

Tamiko took a deep breath. "Sphinx, sunset, walk a hundred paces, hippopotamus, crossed-out sunbeams, a person looking up, and the number twenty," she said.

"Thanks, Tamiko!" said Kiki.

"Thanks, everyone!" Gustavo added. "Beagle out."

"Good luck!" their friends called, then the screen went blank once more. Gustavo hid the communications box under the wooden bench.

BEEP BEEP BEEP! went the Beagle.

"I think it's wishing us good luck too," said Gustavo with a grin. "Thanks, Beagle!"

They jumped onto the shore. "We need to buy some mortar," said Kiki. Then her face fell. "We haven't got any ancient Egyptian money, though."

"They didn't use money," Gustavo said, as they scrambled up the bank towards the pyramids. "They swapped things instead."

"We haven't got anything to swap either," said Kiki.

Gustavo grinned. "We have – the incense Bek gave you!"

They came to a row of small houses.

Some had mats outside where the owner sat with goods for sale. Outside a bigger house, a merchant was stacking building materials. "Let's try him," Gustavo said.

He asked for mortar, and offered the incense in exchange. The merchant's face lit up. "My daughter will love it," he said, handing Kiki a bulging sack. "It's her favourite scent."

The sun was going down as Kiki and Gustavo headed past the Sphinx. They stood

behind it, facing Pharaoh Khufu's pyramid. To Gustavo's dismay, he realised that the men standing around its base were armed with thick, heavy clubs. Several had daggers tucked into their kilts.

"I don't want to see anyone slacking off!" a broad man was yelling at them. He carried a spear. "Don't let anyone near this pyramid!"

"Oh no!" said Kiki. "How can we get in without being seen?"

"We'll think of something," said Gustavo,

and then he felt his heart sink. Heading towards the boss guard was Nebet. Yuf stumbled along after her, clutching a large bundle of poles. Bunefer followed – she had a coil of rope over her shoulder

and a pottery lamp in her hand. Kiki grabbed Gustavo's arm and pulled him into the shadow of the Sphinx, where they were out of sight.

Nebet's voice carried in the still air. "Officer, I'd like you to make the guards go away."

The boss laughed. "Oh, you would, would you? And I'd like to be Egypt's next pharaoh!"

"I'm serious," Nebet said. "Will this change your mind?"

She handed him something that sparkled in the setting sun.

"Jewels," Kiki whispered.

The boss grinned. "Guards! Off we go on a nice long break!"

The guards started to march away. The boss guard followed, and called back to Nebet over his shoulder. "Thanks for the jewels! But there's no way you lot will be able to fit through the tunnels, not with all the rubble in there. You're far too big!"

"Kiki, I *think* I know how to get into the pyramid," said Gustavo. "It's risky, though."

"I'm up for anything that will save the museum," Kiki replied. "What's your idea?"

"No time to explain," said Gustavo. "Just trust me."

They walked towards the gang. Gustavo felt jittery with nerves. *I've got to get this right*, he thought.

Nebet's eyes narrowed. "You two again! What do you want?"

Gustavo took a deep breath. "We know you're tomb robbers," he said.

Nebet laughed. "And you think you can stop us, do you?"

"No," Gustavo replied. "We want to help you."

Chapter Five
A RISKY PLAN

Nebet scowled. "Why would you two want to help us? We know you're friends with the mummifier's grandson." She glanced down at the sack of mortar. "And what's that?"

"Er..." said Gustavo. *This isn't going well*, he thought.

To his relief, Kiki stepped in. "Remember

when you stole the papyrus?" asked Kiki. "Well, we were trying to steal it, too."

"Yes, that's right!" said Gustavo. "And this sack of mortar is to... er... seal up the tomb. After we've stolen the treasures, of course."

Kiki nodded. "Then no one will know they've gone. So that means no one will be looking for us robbers, right?"

Nebet's cold eyes flickered from Gustavo to Kiki. Gustavo could see that she still hadn't made up her mind about them. His heart was pounding. *We've got to convince her she*

needs our help!

"That guard was right," he said. "You and your gang could never squeeze past the rubble. But Kiki and I are much smaller. We can do it! All we want in return is a bit of the treasure. Deal?"

Nebet frowned – and then a greedy grin spread over her face. "All right," she agreed. "Deal."

Yuf and Bunefer cheered. "Yeah, yeah, yeah!"

"But just a *tiny* bit of treasure – that's all you'll get," said Nebet. "And I'll be watching you. Make one wrong move..."

"We won't," Gustavo said firmly.

Yuf and Bunefer danced around each other. "Now we don't have to go into the scary pyramid," said Yuf. "These two kids can do it!"

"Silence!" ordered Nebet with a stare. They immediately fell quiet. Nebet reached into the folds of her shawl and drew out the stolen papyrus. She unrolled it. "Now we must find the entrance..." Nebet stared at the hieroglyph code, muttering to herself. Finally she said, "Stupid thing! It doesn't make any sense."

Bunefer peered at it over her shoulder.

"You've probably got it upside down."

Nebet turned the papyrus the other way up, then glared at Bunefer. "Silly fool! Whoever heard of a pyramid with the pointy bit at the bottom!"

"H-have you tried it sideways?" Yuf asked.

Nebet closed her eyes. She looked as if she was about to bite Yuf's head off.

"Let us try," Gustavo said quickly. *Maybe Nebet and her gang can't read*, he thought. He knew that only a small number of ancient Egyptians could.

Nebet passed the papyrus to him. She crossed her arms and tapped her feet on the dusty ground while Gustavo and Kiki examined the hieroglyphs.

Kiki whispered, "Can you remember what Tamiko said they meant?"

"I think so," said Gustavo. "Sphinx, sunset, walk one hundred paces, hippopotamus, crossed-out sunbeams, a person looking up, twenty."

Kiki looked around. "Well, the Sphinx is behind us now. And it's sunset. Let's try walking a hundred paces."

With the robber gang following, Gustavo and Kiki walked, counting as they went.

"Ninety-eight...ninety-nine...one hundred," said Gustavo, stepping on to a low rock that was in his way. He glanced down at the

papyrus. "Next is the hippopotamus. I don't get that. There's no hippo here."

Kiki giggled. "You're standing on it!" she said.

"*What?*" Gustavo quickly looked down, then laughed. The rock he was standing on was shaped exactly like a sleeping hippopotamus.

"Stop messing about," Nebet called. "Get on with it!"

Gustavo checked the papyrus again. "Yellow circle with lines crossed out. Oh, yes – sunbeams." He frowned. "But what does that mean we should do next?"

Kiki thought for a moment. "Maybe it doesn't mean sunbeams... maybe it means where there's no sun... Gustavo, look!"

She pointed to the area in front of the pyramid. It was in deep shadow.

"Amazing, Kiki!" said Gustavo, and they ran over to it.

"Oi! Wait!" shouted Nebet, running after them. Yuf and Bunefer followed her, carrying their ropes and poles.

Gustavo glanced at the papyrus. "Next is the person looking up and the doorways that mean twenty," he said. He looked at the sloping side of the pyramid that rose before them. Excitement bubbled inside him as he

realised what the instructions meant. "Go up twenty blocks! That's where the secret entrance must be!"

"Brilliant!" Kiki clapped him on the back.

Gustavo rolled up the papyrus and tucked it inside his tunic. They began to climb, using the gaps between the polished stones as hand and footholds. Gustavo could hear Nebet grumbling and Yuf and Bunefer panting for breath as they scrambled up too. The blocks were huge, and Gustavo thought it was like clambering up a giant's stairway.

After a while, Kiki stopped. "This is the twentieth block," she said.

Gustavo called down to Nebet. "We reckon the entrance must be behind this block."

"Up you go, Bunefer," Nebet said. "You're the strongest. Push the stone aside."

Bunefer passed the lighted torch over to Nebet and scrambled up beside Gustavo and Kiki. She gritted her teeth and pushed the block. Nothing happened.

Nebet frowned. "Go and help her, Yuf," she ordered.

Yuf climbed up too. They both pushed and shoved, then turned and leaned on the block, pushing with their backs. With a loud, scraping noise, the stone block moved. It swivelled sideways, revealing the entrance to a dark tunnel. A mouldy smell wafted from inside.

Nebet climbed up and peered in. Her eyes gleamed. "Soon we'll be as rich as the pharaohs!" She lit the pottery lamp and handed it to Gustavo. "Well, what are you waiting for? In you go."

"We'll need those too," Kiki said, pointing at the bundles of ropes and poles.

Bunefer and Yuf gave them to her so fast that Kiki almost dropped them.

"Glad it's you going in, and not us," said Yuf. "The gods don't like tombs being disturbed."

"Especially Anubis," said Bunefer. "He'll send evil spirits to get you!"

Gustavo shivered.

"Go on," said Nebet. "Go and fetch my treasure!"

Gustavo took a deep breath. Then he and Kiki stepped into the dark tunnel of Pharaoh Khufu's pyramid...

Chapter Six
INSIDE THE GREAT PYRAMID

Gustavo and Kiki made their way along the dark, stuffy tunnel. They had to stoop to avoid scraping their heads on the rough stone ceiling. Apart from the light flickering from the lamp, it was as dark as the darkest night. Gustavo was glad he didn't believe in Bunefer's evil spirits. *If I did,* he thought, ***this would be very creepy.***

The ground sloped steeply downwards and they had to be careful not to slip.

"I thought it would be cold in here," Kiki said. "But the further we go, the warmer it gets."

"You're right," said Gustavo. He could feel his hair sticking to his damp forehead.

The tunnel flattened out and turned a sharp corner. Then it curved to the left and sloped upwards. Ahead, a tall, dark shadow was blocking their way.

"It's rubble left by the pyramid builders," Gustavo said when they reached it. The lamplight showed a huge mound of stones. "It's to stop robbers."

Kiki squashed up beside him. "Do you think it will stop us, too?"

"I'm not sure..." Gustavo held the torch high. "Hey, there's a little gap at the top! Let's see if we can squeeze through it."

Kiki started scrambling up the pile of rubble. Gustavo kept the torch held as high as he could to help her see. Kiki's movements made shadows jump over the walls of the tunnel. Gustavo waited nervously.

"Just... need... to move... some... of these rocks..." Kiki panted when she reached the top of the pile. "So we'll... fit through..." There was a crash as she pushed them off the top of the heap.

Gustavo passed the ropes and poles up to Kiki. She pushed them through the gap she'd made, then held the torch so Gustavo could climb up. His sandals slipped on the rocks, but soon he was at the top of the heap of rubble.

"I'll go first," he said, and wriggled into the

gap Kiki had made.

Gustavo felt hot and cramped as he crawled along the top of the rubble, trying not to scrape his head on the tunnel roof. He held the torch in one hand and pulled himself along with the other. "It's tight," he called back to Kiki, "but we can fit through!"

He could hear Kiki starting to crawl after him, pushing the poles and ropes ahead of her. Gustavo was sweltering from the effort. He couldn't help giving a "Whoop!" of relief as he reached the other side of the rubble heap and scrambled down to the ground. Kiki passed him the ropes and poles and jumped down next to him.

"We did it!" said Gustavo. Then he saw that Kiki looked very fed up. "What's up?"

"Look at that," she said. She pointed ahead of them.

Gustavo groaned. The light from the lamp flickered over a blank wall. "All that effort," said Gustavo, "and it's a dead-end."

Kiki laughed nervously. "Well, it is a tomb."

Gustavo moved the torch from side to side. "Hey! It's not a dead-end – it's a junction! The tunnel carries on around both corners."

"Which way should we go?" wondered Kiki.

Gustavo peered in each direction. "I think I can see something down here," he said, waving the lamp towards the right-hand tunnel.

They gathered up the poles and ropes and set off down a slope. Gustavo gasped. The thing he'd seen was a white-painted doorway. It was covered in brightly coloured hieroglyphs.

"The King's Chamber!" he whispered.

They peered through the doorway and saw a huge carved stone box.

"The Pharaoh's sarcophagus!" said Gustavo. "It's a kind of coffin. Just think, Khufu's mummy is inside that."

"A real pharaoh!" whispered Kiki. "What

are those?" She pointed to several containers next to the sarcophagus.

"Canopic jars!" Gustavo said excitedly. "They hold bits of his body that were removed before it was mummified." He was trembling with excitement. Their eyes roved over jewelled chests, golden bowls and cups, baskets of food, jewels, and even games. There were beds and chairs for servants to carry the pharaoh upon.

"Everything Khufu needs in the afterlife," Gustavo said in wonder. He lifted the torch higher. "Look at all the treasure!"

Scattered around the tomb were a collection of incredible

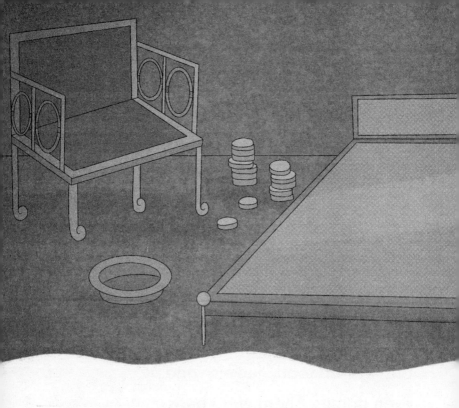

objects. There was a bed with a golden canopy, a carrying chair, and thrones covered in gold and jewels.

He noticed some little stone statues standing around the sarcophagus. "Look – shabti figures," he told Kiki. "They're servants. The ancient Egyptians believed they would work for the pharaohs in the afterlife."

Kiki was examining hieroglyphs on the doorway. "Bek could read these," she said. "I wonder what they say."

"They're probably curses, warning thieves to keep out," Gustavo said. "Come on, we mustn't forget the plan! Let's start shifting rubble to the treasure chamber entrance, so we can build a wall."

Back at the junction, Kiki wedged the torch into a gap between stone blocks. She sorted through the poles until she found what she wanted. She looked around until she spotted large cracks high up on each wall. Using the cracks to jam the pole across the tunnel, she flung a rope up so it hung over the pole.

"Tie that end of the rope around a chunk of rock," she said to Gustavo. "I'll pull on the other end, and you can use a pole to push the rock free."

Gustavo did as she asked. As Kiki pulled the rope, he leaned all his weight on the end of the pole.

CRRRRRRKKKK! The rock moved.

"Again!" said Kiki.

The stone shifted free. Gustavo helped Kiki swing it onto the slope that led to the

King's Chamber. The rock rumbled down towards the door.

"Wow!" said Gustavo. "That's a big lump of rock, but we moved it pretty easily."

"That's because we're using the pole as a lever," Kiki explained. "It's doing the work for us." She grinned. "You're not the only history expert around here," she teased. "Did you

know the ancient Egyptians invented levers
and ramps for moving heavy objects?"

"Cool!" said Gustavo.

They carried on shifting rubble as fast as
they could.

"We'll soon have enough to block off the
chamber entrance," Gustavo said. "That'll
keep Nebet and her gang out!"

"I knew it!" shrieked a voice, echoing

around the tunnels.

They both froze with horror. It was Nebet!

Kiki's eyes were wide. "She's on the other side of the rubble pile," she whispered.

"Yuf! Bunefer!" Nebet yelled. "Those kids aren't helping us – they're trying to stop us! After them!"

Gustavo grabbed the torch. "Come on, Kiki! Let's run!"

Chapter Seven
TRICKING THE ROBBERS

Gustavo and Kiki sprinted down the left-hand tunnel. It was so narrow that Gustavo could feel his arms brushing the stone walls.

"Get a move on, Yuf!" Nebet's voice echoed. "If Bunefer and I can squeeze over this rubble, so can you."

"They're using the gap we made," said Kiki with dismay.

Then came the crash of falling rocks, a whimper from Yuf, and the sound of lots of pounding feet.

"Quick!" Gustavo said. "They're coming this way!"

Ahead, the torch showed a large alcove in the tunnel wall.

"Here!" Gustavo whispered, pulling Kiki inside the small, cramped space.

"The lamp!" Kiki said. "They'll see us!"

Gustavo dropped the lamp and kicked dust inside it. They were left in total darkness. It was so black that Gustavo couldn't even see the wall. He touched Kiki's shoulder. "Are you okay?" he whispered.

"It's really scary." Her voice shook. "You?"

"It's horrible," he said. "I never imagined anywhere could be this dar–"

He broke off. A light glowed in the blackness.

The light grew brighter. It was Nebet, holding another lamp. It lit up her angry face. She and Bunefer ran past their hiding place, with Yuf puffing along behind. Gustavo's heart pounded so loudly, he was worried they would hear it.

But they didn't. As the gang's footsteps died away, he heard Kiki take a deep, shaky breath.

"Whew!" she said. "We've given them the slip. For now, anyway."

"And we've still got a mission to complete," Gustavo said.

"Right," said Kiki. "Let's try to go back the way we came."

They tiptoed back along the dark tunnel. Kiki kept one hand on Gustavo's shoulder, so they wouldn't get separated. Gustavo felt his way along the wall. He could see nothing but blackness.

Nerves fluttered inside him. *Anything could be waiting for us,* he thought.

FLASH!

A glowing light shone ahead. It lit up the tunnel, dazzling them in the sudden brightness.

Kiki clutched Gustavo's arm. "Nebet's found us!"

"Let's go," Gustavo said. "Quick!"

But then a voice said, "Gustavo? Kiki? Is that you?"

Gustavo blinked. As his eyes grew used to the light, he saw a figure holding a reed torch – and it was too small to be one of the gang. He grinned with relief when he realised who it was. "Bek!"

They rushed to meet him.

"I'm so glad it's you!" said Kiki. "But what are you doing here?"

"I saw the secret door was open, so I came in to try to stop those robbers," said Bek.

The three friends huddled together to decide what to do. Gustavo and Kiki knew their original plan wouldn't work, because the gang would hear them shifting rubble.

"We could scare them away instead," Gustavo suggested. "Just like Bek scared us!"

"But how?" said Kiki. "We don't look scary."

"We don't need to look scary," he said. "Remember Anubis and the bad spirits? I've got an idea that just might work..."

*

"Ready!" said Gustavo.

They were inside the King's Chamber. Around them, the gold and jewels glittered in the light from Bek's torch. Gustavo carefully wedged it between two jars of oil, and ducked down into the shadows. Kiki had rigged up a pulley and was holding the end of a pair of ropes. The other ends were tied around shabti figures.

"Ready!" she called.

Bek was crouched near Gustavo, clutching one of Kiki's incense pellets. "Ready too!" he said.

Gustavo was tense with nerves. He glanced at Khufu's sarcophagus. *I hope you don't mind us being here, Pharaoh*, he thought. *We're trying to save your treasures!*

"They're coming!" Bek hissed.

Gustavo listened. Bek was right – he could hear footsteps outside the chamber and Nebet's cross voice. Then Bunefer gave a yelp. "Treasure!" she screeched. "We've found it!"

Gustavo could just make out the gang all peering through the chamber doorway.

"Wow," said Yuf. "We're rich!"

"As rich as pharaohs," said Nebet. "As long as those kids stay out of the way. Hey, where's that light coming from?"

Bek had picked up the torch, and was dipping its flame to the incense. It lit and he blew on it gently, making smoke rise. Then he tucked the torch back between the jars and scuttled over to Kiki.

Nebet stalked into the chamber, Yuf and Bunefer following. Gustavo gently moved his arms to make the smoke from the incense drift towards the gang.

"What's that?" snapped Nebet.

Yuf and Bunefer looked around nervously. "Smoke," said Yuf. "Ritual smoke. That's not right..."

Kiki and Bek yanked on the ropes.

SCRRRRRRKKKK!
SCRRRRRRKKKK!

Two of the little shabti figures moved along the ground. In the gloomy torchlight, it looked as if they were magically moving all by themselves.

"Yikes!" yelped Yuf.

"Evil spirits!" Bunefer squealed. "Eek! We should never have come here! Run, Yuf!"

They sprinted out of the chamber. Gustavo could hear them scrambling over the rubble pile and racing away towards the secret entrance, their shrieks ringing behind them. He couldn't help grinning!

But Nebet snorted. "Silly kids," she said. "I know it's you. Smelly smoke and a couple of shabti figures don't scare me!" She walked further into the treasure chamber, towards where Gustavo, Kiki, and Bek were hiding. "Come on, show yourselves!"

Oh no, thought Gustavo. *We've only got one trick left. It's our last chance to save the treasures... and the museum!*

Chapter Eight

HELP FROM ANUBIS

Gustavo crouched low to the ground. He was hidden behind a throne, with Nebet marching towards him. He could see Kiki and Bek hiding behind piles of jewels. The light from Bek's torch flickered over their worried faces.

"Where are you?" growled Nebet.

Gustavo put his hands together with his

thumbs sticking up, and held them upright. The torchlight threw the shadow made by his hands onto the wall in front of Nebet. It was shaped just like the head of a jackal.

Gustavo moved his hands forwards. The shadow grew larger.

Nebet stopped and stared, her eyes wide. "Anubis!" she said with a gasp.

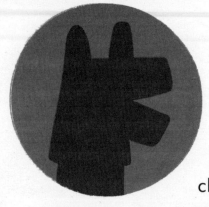

Gustavo moved his fingers like a pair of scissors, so the jackal seemed to open and close its jaws.

Nebet shook so hard her shawl fell from her shoulders. "Please don't hurt me, Anubis!" she shrieked. "I wasn't going to steal anything, honestly!"

She turned and fled. Gustavo heard her scramble over the rubble pile, and then her pounding feet echoed through the tunnel as she raced for the exit.

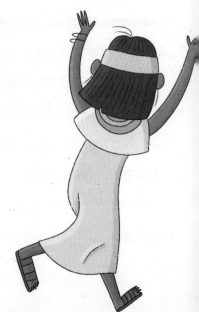

After a couple of moments, the inside of the pyramid was

silent.

"It worked!" Gustavo shouted. "She's gone!"

The cheers of the three friends echoed off the stone walls. Gustavo and Kiki high-fived. "Yay!" shouted Kiki.

Bek looked confused, then stuck his hand up for a high-five as well. He still looked confused after he'd done it!

"Let's seal off that chamber before any of the robbers come back," said Gustavo.

Kiki giggled. "If they dare!"

They carefully placed the shabti figures back where they belonged. Then Kiki showed Gustavo and Bek how to rig up pulleys and levers. It was hard work, but soon they'd shifted almost all the rubble they needed to the doorway.

"Let's get the mortar ready," said Gustavo.

Kiki grabbed the sack, then stopped.

"What's up?" Gustavo asked.

"Water," Kiki said in a small voice. "We need water to mix it and we didn't bring any."

Gustavo groaned. "Oh no!"

But Bek took a stone jar from his bag. "Here," he said.

Gustavo grinned with relief. "Excellent!

Thanks!"

"It's a good thing you sneaked into the pyramid too, Bek," said Kiki.

"Definitely," said Gustavo. "This wouldn't have worked without you!"

They stacked the rubble across the doorway, using the mortar to stick the rocks together. Gradually, Pharaoh Khufu's sarcophagus and his magnificent treasures disappeared from view behind the wall they were building. Between them, Kiki and Bek held Gustavo up on their shoulders so he could slot the last rock into place. He took a last glimpse of the treasure chamber. *I hope no one disturbs it for thousands of years now*, he thought. He fixed the rock in place and the chamber was completely hidden.

Bek put his head on one side. "There's just one more thing," he said, pulling brushes and inks from his bag. He started writing hieroglyphs around the sealed doorway.

"What does it say?" Kiki asked, peering over his shoulder.

Bek grinned. "It's an extra curse," he said. "If you ever meet someone with a bright green nose, very hairy ears and a voice like a hippo with a tummy ache, you'll know he tried to break down our wall!"

Everyone laughed. As they made their way out of the pyramid, Gustavo spotted something familiar in the torchlight. He picked it up.

"Your grandad's papyrus with the secret

directions!" he said. "It must have fallen out of my tunic." He passed it to Bek.

Bek shook his head. "Please can you keep it?" he asked. "If you take it back home to Discoveria, none of the robbers around here will ever get hold of it."

"Of course we will," said Gustavo. He put the papyrus back inside his tunic.

When they reached the outside and the cool night air, there was only a crescent moon. No one noticed the three of them heaving the huge block of stone back over the entrance – with the help of Kiki's levers – and then making their way towards the dock.

"Kiki and I had better go home now," said Gustavo.

"You have a long journey ahead," said Bek. "All the way to Discoveria."

"It is quite a journey," Gustavo agreed, "but it shouldn't take too long." Kiki gave him a grin.

When they reached the Beagle, Bek said, "Thanks for everything you've done. My grandad would be grateful too, if he knew."

"It was a brilliant adventure," said Kiki.

Gustavo made a fist and held it out. "Fist

bump?" he said.

Bek made a fist, too. "Fist bump," he said. "I guess that must mean goodbye..."

When they'd all bumped fists, Gustavo and Kiki jumped aboard the Beagle. Gustavo grabbed the oars, and Kiki set the sail. Bek gave the boat a shove away from the dock, then waved as they moved off.

"Bye, Bek!" Gustavo called.

"You'll be a great scribe!" Kiki added.

Wind filled the sail and they turned to take a last look at the pyramids.

"It's awesome to think we've actually

been inside one!" said Gustavo.

When the pyramids were in the far distance, they changed into their ordinary clothes. They sat on the wooden bench and Gustavo pressed the button on the communications box that was marked "HOME".

Dazzling white light surrounded them. The Beagle rattled and shook as it accelerated to an incredible speed. The light faded, and they came to a shuddering standstill. They were back in the Exploration Station once more, and the Beagle had turned back into an old go-kart. The other Secret Explorers excitedly hurried over.

"Did you stop the robbers?" asked Ollie.

"What's ancient Egypt like?" Cheng asked.

"Did you see inside the pyramid?" Roshni

wanted to know.

Before Gustavo and Kiki could answer, a screen projected up from the floor. It showed the museum they'd seen before, but this time it was packed with visitors. They were looking at a reconstruction of Pharaoh Khufu's burial chamber. Gustavo could see jars, treasures and shabtis. *It's exactly what it looked like!* he thought.

Kiki gasped, and pointed to a wall display

next to the chamber. It was headed, "CURSES! CAN YOU GUESS WHAT THEY SAY?" Beside one curse was a figure with a green nose and hairy ears, and it was clutching its stomach. "Bek's curse," said Kiki with a grin, as the screen vanished.

Gustavo grinned too. Their mission to save the museum had been successful!

"Did you bring anything back for the collection?" asked Leah.

Gustavo carefully pulled the papyrus containing the secret instructions from his pocket. Now it was over four thousand years old, and was faded and fragile.

"I recognise those hieroglyphs," Tamiko

said with a smile. Kiki placed it inside one of the display cabinets.

It was time for Gustavo to go back home.

"What an amazing mission!" Kiki said. She stuck out her fist at exactly the same time as Gustavo high-fived. They both burst out laughing.

"Bye, Kiki!" said Gustavo. "Bye, everyone! See you on our next mission!"

He stepped through the glowing door. The wind whirled him through brilliant white light. When it faded, he stepped out of the lift and back into the Rio de Janeiro museum. Visitors bustled around him, looking at the exhibits. *The museum in Cairo will be this busy too*, he thought happily.

"Excuse me!"

Gustavo turned to see a smiling elderly man and woman.

"We heard that some of the artefacts in the next gallery are on loan from a museum in Egypt," said the woman. "We were wondering if you could tell us about them."

Gustavo grinned. "Of course," he said. "I happen to know a few things about ancient Egypt!"

THE GREAT PYRAMID OF GIZA

The ancient Egyptians believed that life continued after death. They built pyramids to contain the mummified bodies of their kings – the pharaohs. The mummies were meant to stay in the pyramids forever, while the pharaohs' spirits travelled to the afterlife. There are more than 100 pyramids across Egypt. The biggest is the Great Pyramid of Giza, which is near Cairo. It was built for Pharaoh Khufu.

The stone at the top of a pyramid is called the capstone

Burial chamber of Pharaoh Khufu

The outer layer was made of smooth, white limestone slabs

Rough, dark limestone blocks were used for inner structure

FACT FILE

△ Like all the other important tombs of ancient Egypt, it was built on the west bank of the River Nile. The Egyptians believed this was the land of the dead.

△ The Great Pyramid was built in 2589 BCE – that's more than 4,500 years ago!

△ The Great Pyramid is 147m tall and made of 2,300,000 blocks of limestone.

△ It took 20 years to build.

Each block weighed as much as an average elephant!

WHO WAS PHARAOH KHUFU?

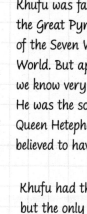

Khufu was famous for building the Great Pyramid, which is one of the Seven Wonders of the World. But apart from this, we know very little about him. He was the son of Sneferu and Queen Hetepheres I, and is believed to have had three wives.

Khufu had the biggest pyramid, but the only surviving statue of him is tiny – just 7.5cm high.

HOW TO MAKE A MUMMY

The Egyptians believed in an afterlife where they would be reborn as spirits, but only if their bodies were preserved as mummies. Only very rich people could afford this, and it took at least 70 days to mummify a pharaoh. Before reaching the afterlife, the spirits of the dead were thought to travel through an underworld called Duat.

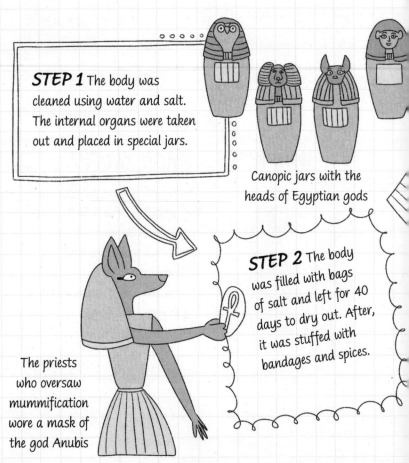

STEP 1 The body was cleaned using water and salt. The internal organs were taken out and placed in special jars.

Canopic jars with the heads of Egyptian gods

STEP 2 The body was filled with bags of salt and left for 40 days to dry out. After, it was stuffed with bandages and spices.

The priests who oversaw mummification wore a mask of the god Anubis

STEP 3 The body was then coated with gum and wrapped in linen strips. Tucked among them were special objects that were meant to protect the dead person in the afterlife.

Heart scarab

Shen ring

Eye of Horus

Mummy wrapped in linen

STEP 4 The mummified body was placed in a decorated stone coffin called a sarcophagus. The sarcophagus was placed inside a tomb.

Some sarcophagi were made from granite and were really heavy

ANIMAL MUMMIES!

The Egyptians mummified animals too, including cats, crocodiles, fish, baboons, and birds. These animal mummies were offerings to the gods, but were also to make sure beloved pets would journey to the afterlife.

GODS AND GODDESSES

Atum-Ra

The father of the gods. Egyptians believed that Atum-Ra created himself and then everything else. He was also one of the gods of the Sun.

GOD OF CREATION

Tefnut
GODDESS OF WATER

The daughter of Atum-Ra. Tefnut represented precious water. She was fierce and had the head of a lion.

Horus
GOD OF KINGSHIP

Each new Egyptian pharaoh was believed to be Horus in a different form. He was shown with a falcon's head wearing the crown of Egypt.

Geb
GOD OF EARTH

Geb represented the earth. He was often shown lying flat to support Nut, who represented the sky. The Egyptians believed that earthquakes were caused by Geb laughing.

Ancient Egyptians worshipped gods and goddesses. Some had the heads or bodies of animals. All of the forces of nature, such as the Sun, storms, and floods, were represented by a god or goddess.

Osiris
GOD OF THE DEAD

Osiris was Egypt's first king. When he died, he became ruler of the dead and decided who could join him in his underworld kingdom.

Isis
GODDESS OF LIFE

Isis was a powerful magician and one of Egypt's most popular goddesses. She represented magic, fertility, motherhood, death, healing, and rebirth.

Nut

GODDESS OF THE SKY AND STARS

Nut's body was home to the stars and the Sun. She was usually shown stretched above Geb.

Anubis
GOD OF EMBALMING

Anubis looked after the bodies of the dead. He created the first mummy, from the body of Osiris. He had the head of a jackal, a type of wild dog.

QUIZ

1   What do you call ancient Egyptian writing?

2   Which massive Egyptian statue had a lion's body and a human's face?

3   The pyramids were built on the bank of which river?

4   What were shabti figures?

5   How long did it take to mummify a pharaoh?

6   What was papyrus made from?

7   What was the name of the stone coffin a mummy was placed inside?

8   Which god had a jackal's head?

SEARCH FOR SCARABS!

There are eight hidden scarabs to spot in this book. Can you find them all?

They look like this!

Check your answers on page 127

GLOSSARY

AFTERLIFE
A second life that some people believe will happen after they die

AMULET
A lucky charm to protect its owner from evil

ANCIENT EGYPT
The period between 3100 and 30 BCE, when Egypt was ruled by pharaohs

CANOPIC JAR
A special jar used to store a mummy's body organs

HIEROGLYPHS
An ancient Egyptian system of writing based around symbols

KHUFU
The pharaoh responsible for building the Great Pyramid of Giza

LIMESTONE

A type of rock that was the main building material in ancient Egypt

MORTAR

A type of paste that builders use to glue rock together

MUMMIFICATION

The process of making a mummy

MUMMY

A body that has been preserved and wrapped in linen

NILE

A huge river that runs through the length of Egypt

PAPYRUS

Name of the green marsh plant and the paper made from its stalks

PHARAOH

The title given to the rulers of ancient Egypt

PYRAMID

A four-sided triangular building with a pointed top, used for burying dead pharaohs

SARCOPHAGUS

A stone coffin containing a mummy

SCROLL

A roll of papyrus containing writing or symbols

SHABTI

Small servant statue that worked for its owner in the afterlife

SPHINX

Mythical creature with a human head and a lion's body

TOMB

A monument or building where the body of a dead person is laid to rest

Quiz answers

1. Hieroglyphs

2. The Sphinx

3. The Nile

4. Servants

5. At least 70 days

6. Reeds

7. Sarcophagus

8. Anubis

For Eddie Beard

Text for DK by Working Partners Ltd
9 Kingsway, London WC2B 6XF
With special thanks to Valerie Wilding

Design by Collaborate Ltd
Illustrator Ellie O'Shea
Consultant Angela MacDonald

Acquisitions Editor Sam Priddy
Senior Commissioning Designer Joanne Clark
Senior Production Editor Nikoleta Parasaki
Senior Producer Ena Matagic
Publishing Director Sarah Larter

First published in Great Britain in 2020 by
Dorling Kindersley Limited
One Embassy Gardens, 8 Viaduct Gardens,
London, SW11 7AY

A CIP catalogue record for this book
is available from the British Library.
ISBN: 978-0-2414-4226-5

Printed and bound in Great Britain by
Clays Ltd, Elcograf S.p.A.

For the curious
www.dk.com

The publisher would like to thank: James Mitchem, and Seeta Parmar
for editorial assistance; Sonny Flynn and Charlie Milner for design assistance;
Caroline Twomey for proofreading.